ETHIOPIAN OPAL

DR. VIKAS SIVADASAN

ISBN 979-888521369-1

Dedicated to my beloved parents

Contents

About The Author

Dr. Vikas Sivadasan, a Keralite spent his childhood in Pilani, Rajasthan, India and Jabalpur, Madhya Pradesh, India.

He did his schooling abroad, in Addis Ababa. After completing 12th Grade, he joined for commercial pilot training. He did Aircraft Maintenance Engineering, BAMS (Bachelor of Ayurveda Medicine and Surgery) and Diploma in Clinical Siddha Practices.

Currently he is practicing as a Medical Doctor (Ayurveda).

Acknowledgements

- Mum - Thanks for your constant encouragement.
- Dad - Thanks for your support and feedback.
- Notion press – Thanks for publishing this book.

Contents

CHAPTER ONE

ALAMAYU PROPOSES MAHLET

It was spring like climate in Addis Ababa. It felt air conditioned like weather and remained that way throughout the year. Addis Ababa, being the capital of Ethiopia, is the focal point of all the transactions. It was also a happening place where embassy of all the foreign countries were located and functioned amicably.

In the heart of the city Bole, lived Alamayu, who was a B. Tech graduate in Metallurgy from Arba Minch University. As he is a B. Tech fresher with no experience, he was jobless and passed his days by loitering around here and there. He had a friend Mangestu who was quite tall, had a bit of dark complexion but very muscular and an excellent basketball player. Alamayu and Mangestu played basketball frequently. They used to spend most of their time playing in the neighborhood basketball court. Alamayu was of average height and physique, had fair complexion and curly hair. Mangestu used to make money by coaching the neighborhood kids' basketball. He used to coach Alamayu without any fee as he was his best friend.

Mangestu soon found a job as salesman in one of the cloth shops in Dembel Mall situated near to the international airport at Bole. Dembell Mall was owned by the famous Ethiopian runner Kebede, who always won gold medal for running in the Olympiad. He was the pride of Ethiopia but was very down to earth and once in a while comes for running with the common folks of Ethiopia, just for fun, at Bole. Now that Mangestu was earning more from being a salesman at the mall, he took Alamayu for lunch at an Indian restaurant Sangam. Alamayu and Mangestu found the Indian cuisine dishes very delicious and had plenty of Indian food like Indian tandoori chicken, butter Nan, butter chicken curry etc., till they were full. Alamayu felt it tasted like Ethiopian injera with doro wat (chicken curry) but was very spicy. After lunch, they had a few drinks at the Sangam hotel bar and were on their way home.

Alamayu's father was ill as he was suffering from terminal lung cancer and almost bedridden. His mother is a secretary at the U.N. and the sole bread winner of the family. Alamayu fed his father supper, did the dishes and went to sleep.

Next day morning, he met Mangestu and his fellow basketball players at the neighborhood basketball court. When they were about to start their game, he noted someone park an SUV car next to the basketball court. A charming and angel like girl stepped out of the car with her poodle dog. She was walking her dog on the pavement next to the basketball court. Alamayu instantly fell in love with her. She was an Ethiopian damsel with curly hair and fair skin.

Alamayu took Mangestu aside and told, "Please let me win the game in front of her. I want to woo her."

Mangestu agreed and made his fellow basketball players allow Alamayu to win the game. He then came to the pavement where she was walking her dog. He said 'hi' to her and introduced himself.

"I am Alamayu. I live only two blocks away. Your good name, please."

She replied, "Mahlet," with a smile.

She continued, "Nice game. By the way, you seem to be very good at basketball."

Alamayu said, "Playing basketball is a piece of cake for me. I actually went easy on the other players or else I could have won and finished the game in just half the time."

Alamayu didn't waste any time in asking her out.

He said, "I have two tickets for the rock concert tomorrow at Sheraton hotel. Would you like to join me?"

Mahlet blushed, and said, "Yes, with pleasure."

Alamayu said, "Great! I will pick you up at 6 PM tomorrow."

He then walked her to her car with her poodle and bid her farewell.

He went back to Mangestu and expressed his thanks.

Mangestu said, "No thanks between friends and way to go man. You got yourself a date in your very first meeting with the girl."

Mangestu added, "Wear something expensive on your first date with her. You know, man, she belongs to the richest family in the neighborhood. Her father owned a chain of five-star hotels in Addis Ababa. She is a spoiled brat of her Dad but is very good at heart."

On his best friend's advice, Alamayu went to Pyasa market, brought the most expensive T-shirt and jeans from a garment shop there with all his pocket money. He patiently waited for the evening; put on the new dress and applied his favorite deodorant, was at her doorstep at sharp 6PM. The front door was opened by Mahlet's Dad. He was huge in size and looked scary.

He asked, "Yes, what can I do for you young man?"

Alamayu said, "Sir I am here to pick your daughter for a rock concert in Sheraton hotel."

He said, "Fine! Mahlet spoke about you, but bring her back on time and no fooling around with my daughter or else I will get you executed."

Alamayu said, "No sir, I will behave extra decent with her and bring her back on time."

Mahlet came out dressed like a model.

She asked, "Dad, did you scare him?"

Her Dad said, "No dear! We were just getting to know each other."

She said, "Okay, bye dad."

Mahlet hooped on Alamayu's bike. He drove in jet speed to impress her all the way to Sheraton hotel. There he showed the free passes he had got for himself and Mahlet to the security. They let them into the concert hall. In no time the concert began. All were dancing to the tunes of electric guitar and rock music. Some were even selling marijuana and L.S.D. as recreational drugs there. Almost everybody was high there and kept dancing nonstop. They were also distributing free booze to rock on in the concert.

Alamayu asked, "Should I get you some beer to drink?"

She said, "No, polite pass."

He was amazed as normally girls of her high society and status usually drink alcohol or at least vodka for that matter. Alamayu and Mahlet danced to the rock music throughout the party. He brought her back home on his bike right on time.

Mahlet kissed him 'goodnight' on his cheek and told him, "I had a good time with you."

Alamayu's spirits were totally lifted up after getting Mahlet's kiss and he was looking forward to meeting her again.

Next day, while playing basketball with Mangestu and his friends, Mangestu asked, "How did the rock concert go with Mahlet?"

Alamayu said, "It was awesome bro! I think I am in love with her."

Mangestu said, "I hope you got her number."

He said, "Yes man," with a smile.

Mangestu said, "Man, propose her before someone else sweeps her off her feet."

Alamayu said, "Never man! "I am on for a date with Mahlet this weekend at Sai Pastry cafeteria. I intend to propose her then and there."

"Good luck bro!" wished Mangestu.

They played basketball till sunset. Mangestu scored most of the time as he was very tall and this gave him advantage over other players. He just had to dunk when he was near the basketball ring and eventually scored every time. By sunset, they were all sweating and went to hit the showers.

Next day, they went for trekking on Simien Mountain which is one of the most beautiful landscapes with mountains and deep valleys. It was formed of huge erosion on the Ethiopian plateau. It's an abode of Ethiopian wolf, Walia Ibex, which is a wild mountain goat, and the Gelada baboon. They continued trekking till afternoon. They had to stop trekking because of the scorching heat of the sun. Alamayu was fully exhausted. They were all famished. They took the packed food from their backpacks to eat.

Mangestu said, "Alamayu, you look emaciated like a T.B. patient after trekking. The packed food in our back packs won't suffice your hunger. You may need the Walia Ibex goat soup to nourish you back to normalcy."

Alamayu said, "Yes, I heard its meat is too delicious and I have been waiting for ages to taste it but it being a threatened species is off limits. Yet, some poachers hunted down Walia Ibex for meat, as it had medicinal values and meat soup was a sure cure for T.B. patients."

One of their friends had a small fracture due to loosing balance on trekking. They took him to a famous Shaman down the valley. The Shaman applied some herbal paste on his legs and bandaged him after repositioning the fractured bone skillfully. After reaching back to Bole, they showed him to Dr. Dassalin in his clinic. Dr. Dassalin was surprised to see that the fracture had already healed.

He said, "The fracture is a surgical case. The Shaman might have some secret knowledge of potent herbs that set right the fracture at once without the need of surgery."

Then, the weekend arrived for which Alamayu was eagerly waiting. He took Mahlet to Sai pastry cafeteria. There he ordered ice creams for both of them. They also had a brownie cake each. They ate slowly as they were totally immersed in each other.

Alamayu commented, "You look gorgeous just like a model. You should seriously think of modelling as a career option."

She blushed, "No thanks, I am more of a homely girl. I have enrolled for attending SAT exam. I hope to crack the SAT exam with flying colors and make it to some college overseas for learning medicine."

Alamayu said, "Good to know that you are a medicine aspirant. It seems you are ambitious. I want to convey my feelings for you before you leave for higher studies."

She said, "Fine! Go ahead, by all means."

He gave her a rose and said, "I love you from the bottom of my heart."

She accepted his proposal and said, "I too love you silly and I was waiting for you to propose."

Then Alamayu took Mahlet for a 3D cinema at Matti multiplex theater. He brought her popcorn. There they saw a romantic movie by sitting next to each other and keeping their hands on each others shoulders and kissed each other intermittently when no one was watching. After the movie was over, he took her back home on his bike. This time she gave him a French kiss as goodnight kiss and waved 'bye' at him.

For Alamayu, it was the happiest day in his life. He then drove his bike, humming romantic songs. He stopped at Fantu supermarket on his way back home. He brought lasagna, vegetables and some grocery items which his mother had told him to bring home. At home, his mother prepared tasty lasagna and served hot in their plates. His mother always used to make mouthwatering lasagna. Alamayu then fed his bedridden father some lasagna, did his daily chores and went to sleep.

In his bed, before sleeping, he dialed Mahlet's phone number covered under his blanket and spoke with her for hours together till midnight and then fell into a deep slumber.

CHAPTER TWO

VISIT TO THE OSTRICH PARK

Next day, a bit around noon, Mahlet asked Alamayu, "Can you accompany me and my sister Bethshabe to orthodox Tawahado church?"

Alamayu said, "With pleasure."

"Don't disclose the matter to anyone in the neighborhood." She said.

Alamayu asked, "What's there to disclose in going to an orthodox church in Ethiopia."

Mahlet said, "This is no ordinary church. The Tawahado church had many holy water sites. This holy water has amazing healing power. My sister Bethshabe and her husband didn't have kids for ten years of their marriage. She hopes to get cured of infertility with the church's traditional healing practice. They had cured many couples of their infertility with the power of holy water and Holy Spirit."

Alamayu agreed and took them to Tawahado church. After praying in the church and experiencing the traditional healing practice of the church with the holy water, they were back in the evening, at Bole.

To everyone's amazement, Mahlet's sister Bethshabe became pregnant within two months. Bethshabe thanked Alamayu for taking them to Tawahado church.

He said, "Thank the lord Almighty and not me. Praise the Lord."

Bethshabe also said, "Yes, praise the Lord. Hallelujah."

From then onwards, Mahlet became very fond of Alamayu. Mahlet made Alamayu join the British council library along with her. The library was abundant with books which explained how to crack SAT exams and TOFFEL exams.

She told Alamayu, "Go through the TOFFEL books. I will read books to clear SAT exams. So both of us can go overseas for higher studies."

"When I undergo medicine degree, you could do your M.S. and join for Ph.D at a nearby college overseas." She said.

Alamayu agreed to her and they became frequent visitors of the British council library. It had branches all over the world. It was well equipped with books to cater to all walks of life. It also had an electronic library, internet café and a general cafeteria upstairs the British council library building. Alamayu and Mahlet, after getting tired reading in the library, used to regularly visit the cafeteria upstairs. Alamayu was very fond of pizza and donuts there. There was a fifty-inch flat screen LED TV installed at the corner of the cafeteria which was tuned to B.B.C channel always. Mahlet and Alamayu made sure they visited the cafeteria every time they went to the library, as they loved munching on pizza and donuts while watching the regular B.B.C channel and occasionally kissed each other when no one noticed.

Mahlet asked, "Do you know why I want to go abroad apart from higher studies?"

He answered, "No, My sweety!"

"I want to check out the Ostrich Park in Australia. The flightless birds, pretty huge in size, will be a treat to the eyes."

Alamayu said, "You don't have to go overseas to check out Ostriches. It is possible to view Ostrich at close proximity in our country, Ethiopia, than anywhere else in the world."

Mahlet was surprised to hear that and she said, "I had no notion of an Ostrich park in Ethiopia."

Alamayu told Mahlet, "I will take you there."

Ostrich Park lies about 207 km south of Addis Ababa. It is located at Lagans Ostrich farm. It is in the Abijata Shalla Lakes National Park. Alamayu and Mahalet went in her SUV to the Ostrich Park. There they were given a warm welcome. The staff of the park allowed them to view the Ostriches from very near. They were also allowed to take pictures with the Ostrich and to touch it with bare hands. Alamayu warned Mahlet to be careful on touching the Ostrich as its legs are quite powerful and Ostriches are known to have killed even lions with their legs. Further, the park staff showed them the Ostrich egg which is the biggest of animal eggs. Ostriches can run at a speed of 70 km per hour. They are the fastest birds on land. Their eyes are bigger than their brain. Eyes are almost the size of a billiard ball. It's about two inches in diameter. Ostrich feathers are used for decorative purposes and as feather dusters. Its skin is used for making leather items. An Ostrich has three stomachs. These stomachs are used to digest the plant matter they consume. Alamayu and Mahlet had a great time there.

On their way back to Bole, in Mahlet's SUV, she said, "I appreciate the way Ostriches are preserved in Ethiopia and taken care of in the park."

Arabian Ostriches in Asia and Arabia were hunted down to extinction. Israel tried to introduce South African Ostriches but failed miserably.

After returning home, when Alamayu went to check on his father, he was shocked to notice that his father had lost his vision. When Alamayu took his father to the nearby hospital, the ophthalmologist said that there is no hope to regain his father's vision. Alamayu still didn't give up hope. Just then, he remembered of the Shaman at Simien valley who had miraculously cured his friend's fractured leg with his herbal knowledge. Alamayu decided to take his father to the Shaman and give a last try. He rented a van and took his father with him to Simien mountain valley.

The Shaman made his father sit on a wooden stool and examined his eyes. The Shaman gave them a Talisman of fire Ethiopian Opal.

The Shaman instructed Alamayu's father, "Wear it all the time. The power of fire Ethiopian Opal will definitely restore your vision in due course."

Alamayu thanked the Shaman, paid him his fees in lump sum Ethiopian Birr and went back home with his father. Within a couple of days, Alamayu's father had regained his eyesight. Alamayu was startled at the drastic improvement of his father's eyesight in such a short span of time.

Alamayu did a research on Ethiopian Opals. He found out that Ethiopian Opal is the latest type of precious opal gemstone mined from the Wollo mines of Northern Ethiopia. The magnificent Ethiopian Opals show an amazing play of colors in multiple patterns. It was discovered in the early 90's. The new Opal variety was found in the mining location of Yita Ridge and Mezezo mines of Shewa province in Africa. After a decade, the Ethiopian Opal gemstones were discovered in the Wollo province in 2008. It has immense internal glow. Ethiopian Opals are known for its astrological as well jewelry purposes. Ethiopian fire Opal, Ethiopian Jelly Opal, pink Ethiopian Opal, blue Ethiopian Opal and black Ethiopian Opal are some magnificent gemstones used for healing and jewelry purposes. Ethiopian Opal is mostly cut and polished to form beautiful cabochons (flat and doomed smooth surface) for making jewelry. Ethiopian Opals with intense color flashes and good transparency are faceted and, therefore, they are of great value.

Ethiopian Opal play of color pattern is usually like ribbon like flashes, honeycomb pattern which often fetch a higher price. Ethiopian white Opal and Black Opal prices are mostly higher than the other color types. The Ethiopian chocolate Opal and fire Opal are also expensive. The Opal has metaphysical properties. The ancient Greeks believed it as a stone of luck and it shields the wearer against negative energy. They believed that it has the power to induce psychic predictions and mystical visions. It intensifies human emotions and frees various inhibitions. These gemstones stimulate the sacral base chakra and cause the kundalini energy to be fully active.

The Romans also believed these Opals as gemstones of immense fortune. Alamayu's mother was all in tears of happiness on seeing her husband regained his eyesight.

She said, "Praise the Lord, I think we should go to Lalibela church and express our gratitude to the Lord, Almighty."

Alamayu's mother was a believer of Lalibela church from childhood as her family was members of the Lalibela church from the very beginning.

Lalibela church is a high place of Ethiopian Christianity. It is a place of pilgrimage. After the Muslim invasion, they prevented the Christian pilgrimages from entering the holy land of Lalibela. After the fall of Aksum Empire, the King of Lalibela built New Jerusalem. Lalibela is around six hundred forty kilometers away from Addis Ababa. The King also made eleven medieval monolithic churches in Lalibela. These churches were marvelously carved out of a single rock.

Alamayu, with his Mom and Dad, went to Lalibela churches. They prayed there with full devotion and thanked the Lord for restoring the vision of Alamayu's father. The people of Lalibela believed that the churches were carved overnight by Angels. Alamayu, with his mom and Dad, returned back home from their religious trip to lalibela and instead of feeling drained with exhaustion, they felt enlightened and fully charged with the divine presence which they felt in the Lalibela church.

ALAMAYU AT WOLLO MINES

Alamayu soon came to know about the vacancy of an engineer at the Wollo mines where precious Ethiopian Opals are being mined on a large scale. He wasted no time in approaching the Wollo mines HR manager with his resume. The manager fixed his appointment with the interview board of Wollo mines. They were impressed with his bio-data and performance at the interview and appointed him as their new engineering supervisor at the Wollo mining site.

On his first day at job, he was amazed to see the Wollo mines infrastructure. Much of the Wollo Opal was produced from a single area of stratified volcanic rocks. The Opal is formed as Silica which contains water accumulated on the top of the impermeable clay. Silica gel got precipitated in the pore spaces of the ignimbrite. Later on, it was transformed into Ethiopian Opal. Horizontal tunnels were made to mine the Opal from the seam that goes along the steep walls of the valley. The ignimbrite is often fractured and poorly lithified. Hence, underground mining was dangerous. The major source of Ethiopian opal was the stratified volcanic deposits which spread over several kilometers. Alamayu was proud to be the engineering supervisor at Wollo mines but was very simple, humble and down to earth and mingled freely with the mine workers. The workers at the mines considered Alamayu as their close friend more than their supervisor. Considering the dangerous nature of mining work there, he gave the workers breaks in between with food and soft drinks supply to keep them nourished and alert all the time at their work. Alamayu's Mom and Dad were also proud of him now that he became an earning member of the family and supported them well. Mahlet was also happy with his success.

Alamayu decided to take Mahlet to the club to celebrate his success in job. The club was shining with beautifully lit multicolored bulbs and chandeliers where they could enter only after flashing thousands of birrs to show the bouncers that they are filthy rich like others who came to the club. The bouncers were huge and muscular, like wrestlers but they generously let them in when Alamayu flashed Ethiopian birrs at them. The DJ at the club played romantic songs at that moment. Alamayu held Mahlet close to him with his arms and they danced romantically to the enchanting romantic beats played by the DJ at the club. They also had a few drinks. Alamayu had Beer and Mahlet was content with the vodka provided at the bar inside the club. They got high and danced for a long while in the club till late night. They enjoyed to the fullest and were back home a little late after midnight. Mahlet's father didn't mind Alamayu bringing her late after midnight as now he had a decent job and thought of him as a good candidate to marry his daughter off.

Alamayu was concerned about the poor livelihood of laborers in the Wollo mines. He ensured that all laborers should get decent wages for their hard work in mining Ethiopian Opals. He also got them hike in their yearly bonus.

The Ethiopian Opals mined at Wollo mines were sold by Ethiopian gemstone sellers in Addis Ababa. Buyers came from all over the world, as investing in Ethiopian Opals had become a new trend everywhere. The sellers provided authentic certificates for Ethiopian Opals. At times, there would be an appraiser to value the exact cost of the Ethiopian Opals. Ethiopian Opals with rainbow like play of color fetched the sellers' lot of money, particularly, the black Opals. Merchants selling fire Opals also acquired good amount of money as fire Opals had medicinal values apart from just ornamental value.

After work, on weekends, he used to have Markyatho (Ethiopian coffee) of top-notch quality at Sai Pastry Cafeteria with his girlfriend Mahlet. They enjoyed Donuts and Croissant along with Markyatho. Ethiopian coffee seeds are considered of the best quality and exported by Ethiopia to foreign countries which generated a lot of money for the country. There is an Ethiopian saying 'Buna dabo naw' which means 'coffee is our bread'. It also implies socializing with others in Ethiopia. People get together for coffee ceremonies where they gossip and also discuss important issues.

As per the legend of coffee in Ethiopia, an Abyssinian shepherd from Kaffa, by the name Kaldi, was herding his goats near a monastery. He saw a sudden change in the behavior of his goats; they started jumping around in excitement. He noted the reason for their excitement was a small shrub with red berries. Kaldi tasted the berries and he also felt the energizing effect of the coffee berries. He filled his pockets with red berries and went home to his wife. She told him to go to the monastery and inform the monks there about the energizing taste of the berries. When Kaldi reached the monastery, his coffee beans were not received well. The monks called it devils' work and threw it into fire. But the aroma of the roasting beans influenced them. They decided to give it a second try. So, they collected the coffee beans from the fire, crushed them and covered them with hot water. All the monks were surprised at the aroma of the coffee and tried tasting it. The monks found the coffees' energizing effect useful in keeping them awake while doing meditation. Therefore, they made a vow to drink it on each and every day of their life. This is how coffee was first discovered in Ethiopia. Mahlet's father was also into coffee plantation business.

Mahlet's father used to cultivate coffee in the region of Yirgacheffe of Sidamo. This area is known for producing the best coffees in the world. He had a wholesale market of coffee seeds at Merkato. From there he exported good quality coffee seeds across the world which made him quite rich. Alamayu used to go with Mahlet to her Dad's wholesale market in Merkato on weekends. On weekends Mahlet helped out her father in business. Alamayu also helped Mahlet's father in assisting his business at Merkato. Merkato being the largest market in Africa, goods making entry into the market were mostly locally grown agricultural products, notably, coffee.

Mahlet soon cleared the SAT exams and got admission in a medical college in Canada. Alamayu was the first person she came to inform about her admission in Canada. Alamayu congratulated her but became gloomy as he knew Mahlet would soon leave to Canada for higher studies leaving him heartbroken in Ethiopia.

Mahlet noticed his sad face and told him, "Honey, if you want me to stay back and marry you instead of going to Canada for higher studies, I will do so with pleasure. You matter to me more than anything else in this world.

Alamayu said, "No worries. You can go, my love."

He insisted Mahlet to go to Canada for higher studies as she is ambitious and very talented. Stopping her from going to Canada is like cutting the wings of a bird in the mid-air which he can never even dream of doing.

Alamayu said, "I am also searching for M.S. admission overseas and would soon catch up with you."

Within a couple of days, Mahlet got her student's visa and was all set to go for medicine graduation abroad. Alamayu brought her a sendoff gift 'a pair of earrings.' She accepted it with delight. Alamayu went along with her parents to send her off at the airport. At the time of departure, Mahlet became emotional and didn't mind crying on Alamayu's chest in front of her parents.

He consoled her, "I will call you daily and e-mail you frequently."

Then she bid farewell to Alamayu and her parents and boarded the Ethiopian airlines flight to Canada.

Mahlet phoned Alamayu right after the plane landed in Canada.

She said, "I had a safe landing in Canada. But I am missing you."

Alamayu told, "Calm down and embrace your career in medicine wholeheartedly. It is the beginning of a turning point in your life. Look forward positively."

Alamayu called her daily from Ethiopia to enquire about her wellbeing.

She said, "I am slowly getting adjusted with the accent here. Canadians mostly speak French which sounded a very poetic language."

Alamayu asked, "What had you learnt in French so far?"

Mahlet told, "I picked up a few words in French like 'Bonjour' for good morning, 'Bosua' for good evening and 'Bonue' for goodnight."

Alamayu told her, "Your voice is very melodious and in French your voice sounds like a lullaby." Mahlet laughed flirtatiously.

Alamayu asked, "How are you finding the Canadian food there?"

She said, "Canadian food is fine but I really missed 'Ethiopian injera' with 'doro wat' and injera firfire."

Alamayu promised her, "I would make delicious 'injera firfire' for you when you come to Ethiopia during your vacation."

Alamayu consoled her by saying, "Mahlet, you are always in my heart though you stay overseas."

Mahlet reciprocated, "I felt the same."

As it was time for her classes, they ended the call.

Alamayu's father's lung cancer was getting worse and the hospital Doctors were charging heavily for chemotherapy which made them practically broken. Alamayu realized that if he doesn't do something about it, he would soon lose his father. One day, while in office, a sinister idea popped up in his mind. The idea was to steal the precious Ethiopian Opal from the Wollo mines, in broad daylight. To Alamayu, it was unethical, as he was a man of principles, but he was left with no other option to save money for his father's chemotherapy and medicine expenditure.

Freshly mined Ethiopian Opals were kept at a nearby store house. Alamayu roped Mangestu in to pull this heist as Mangestu was also in need of some urgent money to pay off his debts. Alamayu made a sketch of Wollo mines and brought it to Mangestu to plan the robbery. Alamayu told Mangestu to be ready with a high-speed car next to the store house where the Ethiopian Opal was kept. Alamayu placed a detonator under the tunnels of Wollo mines. He detonated the bomb with a remote, from a distance, when the laborers where on a lunch break so that no one under the tunnel would get hurt. By hearing the explosion, everyone headed under the tunnel to view the damage caused. Using this distraction, Alamayu opened the storehouse with the keys he had as the supervising engineer of Wollo mines. His eyes glittered with the sight of three to five-kilogram piece of Ethiopian Opal which would fetch him millions. He quickly put it inside his bag and rushed to Mangestu's car. He told Mangestu to drive the car in full speed before anybody catches on to them. By the time, the staff of Wollo mines realized about the robbery, Alamayu had covered a long distance. From the CCTV footage at Wollo mines they found the number plate of the car and informed the Ethiopian police about the robbery. Alamayu told Mangestu to park the car at an isolated place. Alamayu swiftly changed the number plates of the car with fake ones. He also made Mangestu and himself wear fake wigs, moustache and beard so that they should not be recognized until they reached a safe hideout.

Alamayu, on the way, met with an appraiser who assured him that it is a five kilogram Ethiopian Opal worth two million dollars but did not give him a certificate as it was a stolen item. Alamayu dug a hole on the ground behind their neighborhood basketball court and hid the

Opal in a small bag there and covered the hole with mud. He planted a jasmine plant there to remember the Opal's hidden location. Then they remained in one of their old friend's house to stay under the radar of the police. Alamayu went online on his friend's laptop and managed to get an admission for M. tech in India. In the meanwhile, Mangestu arranged for their passports with fake identities to escape overseas.

CHAPTER FOUR

ALAMAYU IN INDIA WITH ETHIOPIAN OPAL

Alamayu went and dug out the Opal and wrapped it in aluminum foil to be undetected by the scanner at the airport. Then they booked airline tickets and straightaway went to board the Ethiopian airlines to Mumbai international airport in India. From there, they booked a flight to Bangalore in SpiceJet airlines. After reaching Bangalore, they hired a taxi to a lodge nearby the Ramaiah Institute of Technology, where Alamayu had got admission for M. tech. They got freshened up in the lodge and then Alamayu went to deal with the formalities at Ramaiah College to be a day scholar M. tech student. He got in touch with a few students there who arranged a paying guest accommodation for them to stay in Bangalore. Initially, they decided to stay low for a while to prevent undue attention to the Ethiopian Opal in their custody. Alamayu, after the classes, was sipping cold coffee at the college cafeteria when the M. tech seniors of the college tried to rag him. As Alamayu was not aware of the concept of ragging in India, he thought they were some hooligans trying to manhandle him and gave them the beating of their life. Those students went limping away with bruises all over them from the cafeteria.

Next day, they turned up in the college wrapped in bandages to cover their wounds. They said sorry to Alamayu and shook hands with him as they thought it is better to be friends with the Ethiopian than getting beaten to pulp. Alamayu was finding it difficult to follow the teachings of the professors who taught M. tech, as Indian English accent was slightly different from Ethiopian English. He gradually got accustomed to the accent of Indian English and started following the classes. The Indian professors gave them lots of assignments every now and then. He was getting overloaded with M. tech studies. Moreover, he came to know that he had to submit thesis and do a lot of research under the professors to get his M. tech completed on time. But Alamayu's real intention to come to India was to find a buyer for his Ethiopian Opal so that he could become quite rich and save his father's life.

In the weekend, Alamayu and Mangestu went to MG Road and Brigade Road in Bangalore for shopping. They were amazed to see the city so hi-tech resembled mini Canada or America. It was filled with foreigners from different countries apart from some local Bangaloreans. They noted a Nigerian bargaining for a DVD player and Woofer set with speakers. They were happy to see a fellow African in Bangalore. They introduced themselves to the Nigerian and asked the Nigerian about his nature of work in Bangalore.

The Nigerian said, "My name is Ekong and I am into smuggling A-grade quality drugs from Nigeria to India."

He further told, "I could get you hooked on to drugs as and when you want."

Alamayu said, "No thanks, but we will be very grateful if you find a buyer for our five-kilogram Ethiopian opal."

The Nigerian was shocked to hear that they were in possession of a five kg Ethiopian Opal.

He said, "People get killed for this kind of stuff here. Do you have a certificate for the opal from an authorized appraiser?"

Alamayu said, "No we don't have certificate but an appraiser had valued it to be around two million dollars worth five kg Ethiopian Opal."

Ekong laughed and said, "Without a certificate, you won't be able to sell it in any jewelry shop as merchants would demand for a certificate to verify the authenticity of the Opal. But I would try to sell your Opal in the black market. But you will have to settle for lesser amount than two million, without the certificate."

In order to do so he wanted fifty percent share of the sale money. Alamayu and Mangestu discussed with each other for a minute.

They told Ekong, "We are ready to share thirty percent share of the money and that too if we received the full amount in white money."

Ekong said, "Alright man! You Ethiopians drive a hard bargain."

He asked for Alamayu's phone number and said, "I would contact you as and when I am ready with a deal for you in the black market."

Meanwhile, Alamayu continued attending his M. tech classes with full dedication and Mangestu used to spend the days drinking beer in the paying guest house. Mangestu used to hide the beer bottles under his cot as it was prohibited to drink and smoke in the paying guest house. Days passed but Ekong didn't call them.

So Alamayu decided to request the house owner whether he could get in touch with some localites who would know where to sell their Ethiopian Opal. The house owner was a fat Bangalorean Brahmin with a thick moustache. He took sympathy on them and said that he has a jewelry merchant friend who would know where to sell this Opal.

He said, "I will consult with my friend and get back to you."

Alamayu and Mangestu saw a ray of hope in their owner's eyes and were waiting impatiently for a positive reply. Same day evening, he called Alamayu and Mangestu who were living as paying guests on the upper floor of their house.

He said, "My merchant friend had emphasized that he could only get you a deal for the Ethiopian opal if you had procured a certificate for your Opal from a licensed appraiser verifying the authenticity and value of the Opal."

Alamayu, to his disappointment, said, "We have no such certificate."

The house owner said, "Sorry, then I cannot be of any help to you."

Alamayu still had faith in God and believed something would soon turn the table to their side. Mangestu became heart broken.

Alamayu told Mangestu, "Have patience man!"

He continued attending his M. tech classes coolly. On a Sunday afternoon, the house owner's son went to play in their house garden and came very late for lunch. His mother scolded him for being late for lunch. He kept mum, ate his food in pindrop silence and went to his room and locked it from inside. The house owner's kid's name is Arav and he is twelve years old. He is pretty shy and an introvert kid in nature. As the kid lay on his bed to sleep, his cot started shaking. Arav looked under his cot and found nothing. Again, when he tried to sleep, the cot started levitating in the air. Arav tried to get out of the cot but his body was stuck on the bed and he couldn't move. Arav started screaming for help. His mother came hearing him scream but couldn't open the door as it was locked from inside. She called Alamayu and Mangestu for help.

Mangestu broke the door open with a kick on the door with his long legs. They got in but were shocked to see Arav stuck on the cot levitating in the mid-air. His mother prayed to God for mercy. The windows of the room got opened by itself. A strong wind gushed into the room. All things in the room started falling apart. Alamayu and Mangestu tried to pull the cot down from the air. With great difficulty, Alamayu and Mangestu pulled the cot down to the floor. Alamayu closed the windows. Arav was no more stuck on his bed and ran to his mother crying. Alamayu and Mangestu were frightened to see such bizarre phenomena happening in the house. Arav's mother thanked them.

Alamayu and Mangestu went upstairs. They didn't speak for a while.

After sometime, Mangestu said, "I think the kid is possessed."

Alamayu told him, "Keep quiet. Don't scare the house owner."

The house maid told Arav's mother, "I am sure, this is the doing of some evil spirit. I know a black magician who can free the house, of the evil spirit."

Arav's mother told her, "Will you shut up? Black magic and evil spirits are superstitions. Never speak about this rubbish further to anyone."

When Arav's father came home in the evening from work, his mom told him about what they had gone through.

Arav's father laughed at her and said, "It might be the wind or a small earthquake that might have shaken Arav's cot. Relax and forget about it."

At dinner time, Arav behaved quite normally and ate his food. He wished 'goodnight' to everyone and they all went to sleep.

At midnight, Arav's parents' sleep was broken by the loud screaming of a monkey. Arav's father went to check outside. To his horror, he found Arav biting the neck of a monkey and drinking its blood. Arav's father immediately separated Arav and the monkey. Arav was drenched with the monkey's blood. Arav's father slapped him hard and made him to shower and change his dress. He then felt guilty for having slapped his son.

He said, "Sorry, dear. What led you to drink the blood of a monkey?"

Arav said, "I don't remember anything."

"I was sleeping on my bed. The next moment I was standing drenched in monkey's blood when you slapped me." Arav said.

Apart from that he remembered nothing of the incident.

Arav's father consoled him, "It was a nightmare. Go and sleep."

He tugged him to bed and placed a book of Gita under Arav's pillow and assured him that it is safe to go to sleep.

Arav's father told his wife about their son's strange behavior.

He said, "I think we should go to the Vishnu temple and pray for our son's wellbeing."

Next day, morning Arav's parents went to the Vishnu temple and prayed for their son's wellbeing. They spoke about their son's strange behavior to the temple priest. The priest assured that he will pray for their son's health. They returned home early itself.

As usual, Arav's father went to work. He was a supermarket owner. At the supermarket, Arav's father was finding it difficult to supervise the market that day, as he was totally disturbed by his son's condition. Back at home, Arav's Mom was busy cooking when Arav woke up from sleep. He went to the bathroom to brush his teeth and looked at the mirror. In the mirror he saw his face turn into a skull. He screamed at the top of his voice. His Mom rushed to check on Arav. Arav was sitting at the corner of the bathroom, totally petrified, with his hands closed on his eyes. He was in utter shock. He was not opening his eyes even when his mother asked him what had happened.

When she insisted a lot, he opened his eyes and told her, "Mom, I saw a skull instead of my face in the mirror."

His mom checked the mirror. It seemed okay.

She told Arav, "Stop day dreaming. Go and study something."

Arav's mother was completely upset in the kitchen. Their maid servant mopping the kitchen saw Arav's distracted mother.

She took pity on her and told her, "It seems that someone had done black magic on Arav. I know a Hindu temple priest who could undo the black magic done on Arav."

Arav's mother waited for her husband to be back home. She told him about the temple priest and the maid servant's version of black magic done on Arav. Arav's father agreed to bring the temple priest home to examine Arav.

The priest came after sunset. He came with his two disciples. He kept his hand on Arav's head and claimed to have sensed black magic done on him. He brought a holy compass and pointed it at Arav. The needle started rotating at high speed and stopped at a direction pointing at their house garden. He commanded both of his disciples to start digging in that direction in the garden. After digging a while, they found a skull with two ulnar bones. He told them to get rid of it and to dispose it by burning it into ashes.

The holy priest told them, "Your son is now free of the influence of black magic done on him."

Arav's father thanked the priest and gave him a handsome amount of money as his fees.

For a few days everything went well. Then, at around midnight, Arav started sleepwalking. His Mom caught hold of him and made him sleep on the bed and shut the door to prevent him from sleep walking again from his room. Next day morning, Arav had not come for breakfast. His Mom called Arav a couple of times. When she didn't get any response from him, she went towards Arav's room. The door was locked from inside. She called for her husband. They had to force open the door. They were totally shocked to see Arav's body twisted from all sides like someone had tied a knot using his body. Arav remained stiff at his twisted state of body and kept speaking gibberish. Arav's mother called her sister who was a catholic as she had married a Roman Catholic man.

Arav's mom requested her sister, "Can you get help from your church priest to help my son Arav?"

She requested the church priest for his help.

The priest said, "Your sister's son is possessed by an evil spirit. The only way to save him is to perform an exorcism which required permission from Vatican. It would take some time."

Meanwhile, Arav's parents brought home all sorts of doctors but they couldn't even diagnose his condition. The church priest called Arav's Mom and told her that they are ready to do the exorcism. The priest came along with his verger to perform the exorcism.

The priest told Arav's parents, "When I read the holy Bible, Arav will come out of his twisted position and try to attack me. At that time, you should tie Arav with the help of my verger and confine him to bed to complete the exorcism."

The priest opened the bible and started reading from the Old Testament. Slowly Arav started coming out of his twisted position. He then pounced on the priest and tried to suffocate him to death by pressing his neck with his bare hands. Arav's grip was too tight for a twelve-year-old kid. With great effort, Arav's parents and the verger pulled Arav's hands from the priest's neck and tied him to bed. The priest then pulled a bottle of holy water from his robe and sprinkled the holy water on Arav. Arav again started shouting gibberish to the priest. The priest made a marking of the holy cross on Arav's forehead with holy water. The priest then recited the 'Lord's Prayer' aloud which made Arav fall unconscious.

The priest said, "Evil spirit left Arav's body. He will be perfectly fine when he wakes up next day morning."

As the priest told, when Arav woke up next day morning, he was feeling very fresh. He wished his parents 'good morning.' He behaved perfectly normal for a week. One sunny afternoon, when Arav was taking bath under the shower, suddenly the water from the shower turned into blood. Arav started shouting loudly. Arav's Mom and Dad came running, wrapped him in a towel and asked him what had happened.

Pointing to the shower Arav cried, "Mom, Dad, the shower water had turned into blood."

When his parents looked at the shower water, it was pure water and there was no blood around. They wiped Arav off the water and dressed him and put him to sleep on the bed. One of their neighbors told them that this all could be happening to Arav because there could be some Vastu fault and that they should consult a Vasthu expert. Arav's father straightaway brought a Vasthu specialist to the house.

The Vasthu specialist went inside all their rooms and said, "This house was not constructed as per Vasthu Shastra. So, the flow of energy in this house had turned negative. You have only two solutions, one is to rebuild the house as per Vasthu Shastra or to change your house."

Arav's parents were very much depressed as Arav's father had spent a lot of money building his house like a villa. He couldn't even imagine leaving his house and staying elsewhere. Alamayu had overheard their conversation with the Vasthu expert. He felt sympathy for the house owner.

He approached the house owner with his Ethiopian Opal and explained to him, "This Opal is not only used for ornamentation but it also has immense medicinal values. It has the power to dispel negative energy and to maintain the normal flow of energy around."

Alamayu offered, "I can give you a small piece of the Ethiopian Opal which is to be made into a talisman. Your son, Arav, should wear it at all times. This will protect him from any sort of negative energy influence."

The house owner thanked Alamayu for his help and did accordingly.

Ever since Arav started wearing the small piece of Ethiopian Opal as talisman, everything was back to normal in his house including himself.

Arav's father thanked Alamayu again and said, "I am very grateful to you for saving my son's life. Is there anything I can do for you?"

Alamayu requested him, "Please help me out in selling the Ethiopian opal."

The house owner said, "Fine! I will do the needful."

CHAPTER FIVE

EFFORTS TO SELL THE OPAL

The house owner contacted his high-profile friends regarding the Opal. One of his friends told him that he knew a Gujrati industrialist who is in the habit of collecting antiques and precious stones like the Ethiopian Opal. They fixed a meeting between the industrialist and the Ethiopians. The industrialist arrived by flight, stayed in the five-star hotel Hilton in Bangalore.

The industrialist Ratanlal said, "I am exhausted of the flight journey. I need to rest. I will meet you on the weekend."

Ratanlal was very superstitious. He had hired a private astrologist whom he consulted every now and then for making business deals and for investing money in the share market.

The Ethiopians were on time at the Hilton Five Star - Hotel in the weekend. Before meeting Ratanlal, they had to face his bodyguard. His bodyguard was very huge and muscular. After thorough checking, he cleared them to meet the industrialist Ratanlal. He was an obese man in his fifty's.

He welcomed them to his room and greeted them, "Danana."

Ratanlal said, "I am a big fan of your Ethiopian culture. I heard Ethiopian Opal brought luck to whoever wore it in the form of a ring or necklace. But first things first, I will start a radio conference with my astrology Guru on my laptop kept on the teapoy. You will have to hold the Ethiopian Opal close to the laptop's camera for it to be examined by my Guru."

He started the video conference on his laptop. A Guru with long white beard in orange robe appeared on the screen.

He told the Ethiopians "Hold the Opal close to the camera."

After viewing it for a minute, he ended the conference call from his side and called on Ratanalal's personal phone.

He picked up the phone and said, "Namaste Guruji."

They talked for a while after which he cut the call.

He faced the Ethiopians with a gloomy face and told them with disappointment, "My astrology Guru told me that white Opal is preferred in making astrological predictions over the fire opal which you had in possession. I am very sorry that I am not in a position to buy the Ethiopian Opal. My Guru denied me to do so."

Disheartened, both Alamayu and Mangestu returned to their paying guest house. Alamayu told the house owner about their failed attempt in selling the Opal to industrialist Ratanlal.

The house owner told them, "Don't give up. I will soon find someone else to buy the Opal."

Alamayu and Mangestu became friends with Arav. Mangestu and Alamayu taught Arav basketball and they played basketball on a daily basis. Mangestu coached Arav to be a basketball sharp shooter. Arav quickly learnt to make three pointer basketball shots without missing at the basketball court in their household garden that Arav's father built for them to play and maintain their physique.

The house owner called Alamayu and Mangestu for tea downstairs. He told them about a famous magician by name Garud, who has expressed interest in buying their Ethiopian Opal.

He said, "If you are willing, I can arrange a meeting between him and you guys to make the deal."

Alamayu and Mangestu instantly got ready for the meeting.

The house owner said, "Tomorrow morning, the magician is going to perform levitation right in front of the Forum Mall at Koramangala in the presence of a huge audience. He has invited you both to view his performance. After his performance, he will meet you guys at the five-star Hotel Grand Mercure in Koramangala where he is residing for the time being."

Next day morning, Alamayu and Mangestu reached Forum Mall to see Magician Garud perform live. The area was filled with large number of his fans who were eagerly waiting for magician Garud to levitate in the air. Finally, magician Garud, wearing a white robe and turban, appeared on a small podium they had constructed in front of the Forum Mall. His security kept his fans at a distance from him. He lifted his hands as if to fly and slowly started levitating in the air. He levitated all the way up to the top of the Forum Mall and descended gradually down on the podium. Alamayu, Mangestu and the magician's fans were all dumbstruck by seeing the magician perform such a spellbound feast live in front of them.

After the performance, Alamayu and Mangestu went to meet magician Garud at Hotel Grand Mercure. Once his security had done their complete checking, they were allowed to meet the magician in his room. His secretary invited them to be seated on the couch. She offered them soft drinks and told them to wait for a couple of minutes and that the magician will come to meet them in person, shortly. Alamayu and Mangestu started sipping the soft drinks and when they were about to finish, magician Garud came to meet them. He sat on the sofa in front of them. He was wearing a Raymond suit and beaming with great personality.

Alamayu asked the magician, "How could you levitate so high up in the air without any support?"

Magician Garud said, "A good magician will never reveal his secrets."

Alamyu said, "It was quite an illusion and was very captivating."

The magician smiled and told them, "Show your Ethiopian Opal."

Alamayu opened his bag, showed him the five-kilogram Ethiopian Opal.

The magician said, "There's a legend about the Opal that it is capable of performing astral projections. In the middle ages, it was believed to have the power to grant invisibility to anyone who wrapped the opal in a fresh bay leaf and held it in his hand. I would like to test it."

Alamayu said, "Alright! Please go ahead."

He handed him the Ethiopian Opal. The magician's secretary brought him a bay leaf. He wrapped it in the bay leaf and placed it in his hand for a while but nothing happened.

The magician became upset. He said, "The legend about the Opal granting invisibility seems to be fake. I wanted to use it in my performance to become invisible, but now, as it's not possible, I can't buy your Opal."

By saying this, the magician handed over them back their Opal. Alamayu and Mangestu sadly took their opal but asked for the magician's autograph before they went back to their paying guest house.

After reaching home, Alamayu narrated to the house owner how they were not successful in selling their Ethiopian Opal to the magician.

The house owner said, "It doesn't matter. I succeeded in finding a licensed appraiser who will issue you a certificate for the Ethiopian opal if we give him some extra money under the table."

This gave Alamayu and Mangestu some hope. They went to the appraiser and he issued a certificate for the five-kilogram Ethiopian Opal worth two million dollars. Now, they just had to find a wealthy buyer for the Opal.

The house owner said, "I will try to get your Ethiopian Opal to be part of an auction taking place next week at Bid and Hammer auction house at Jayanagar in Bangalore itself."

On the day of the auction, Alamayu and Mangestu were present at the auction, sitting at the back of the bidders. For bidding, people had come from wealthy families all over India. Some were also present from rich royal families of India to make the bidding. There were a few foreign nationals also to take part in the auction. Various antique pieces were sold which were antique paintings, antique swords, antique jewelry etc. The person auctioning the items for sale spoke loud to open the bidding prices. He hammered and sold the antique pieces to the highest bidder.

Now, it was the turn for their Ethiopian Opal to be sold. The bidding was not going beyond fifty thousand dollars for their Ethiopian Opal. They interrupted the bidding, called their house owner to remove their opal from the auction, as the highest price for their Opal was quite below their expectations and they don't want to sell it at a low price.

When Alamayu and Mangestu had lost all their hope, Nigerian Ekong called them and told, "Be ready with the Opal for sale anytime. I am making a deal for your Ethiopian Opal with the Russian mafia."

Ekong called them again and said, "The Russian mafia boss is at Goa. You have to reach Goa to make the deal with the Russian mafia boss, Vladimir."

Alamayu booked three tickets for them in Vasco Da Gama superfast express train. They boarded the train, reached Goa and stayed in a lodge there.

Alamayu asked Ekong, "How do you know the Russian mafia so well?"

Ekong said, "I used to peddle drugs for them in Bangalore."

Russians used to supply drugs to Bangalore. Their source was the Nigerians there. The cost of one-gram cocaine was above rupees five thousand and LSD costed rupees three thousand. They used to sell these drugs to the elite society. Medical professionals, engineering students and IT professionals were their main target. In addition to this, they targeted various clubs too. Cocaine was available in powder form whereas LSD as tablets in thin sheets. Club goers got addicted to these drugs. Some even die of the over usage of cocaine.

Ekong explained, "We brought these drugs in trains or buses. At a time, we carried about eight hundred grams of drugs. We smuggled it inside our luggage, unnoticed."

Ekong told them, "In Goa, drug business is done in a massive scale. More than eight hundred international charted flights per year made Goa a global selling place for drugs. Not only Nigerians but Israilies are also running drug cartels in Goa. They both have many Goan policemen on their payroll. They were constantly alerted by these policemen when a raid is about to happen. Even if they were caught by the narcotics department, these drugs were resold to them from the police godown. Local politicians supported these drug dealers, as many of the places where they used to supply are owned by them."

Alamayu wondered, "How do they protect them?"

"They protected these drug peddlers by sending them underground from getting deported. Goa turned to be a heaven for tourists due to the happy drug addiction syndrome. The smuggled drugs worth five thousand crore reached Goa by Russians on charted flights and by sea. Some foreigners stay back to manufacture synthetic drugs. The Russian mafia is hidden behind the real estate front. They legalized there stay in Goa by joining partnership with local companies. Russian mafia purchased agricultural land in Goa and turned it into prostitution hubs. They run a sex racket in Goa By trafficking girls from Russia. They sold pure cocaine which could make a person high for two days if consumed." Ekong said.

Alamayu and Mangestu were shocked to hear from Ekong how easily the Russian drug cartel operated their illegal business in Goa with the help of some corrupt politicians and policemen.

Ekong said, "Get ready tomorrow morning at sharp 10:00 AM. The Russian mafia boss Vladimir will reach Goa by charted flight and meet us straightaway."

Alamayu and Mangestu were petrified to meet the Russian mafia boss but somehow build up courage in order to sell their Ethiopian Opal. Ekong took them to a secluded mansion where Vladimir was waiting for them. Vladimir's men were guarding the front entrance with AK-47 guns. The guards checked them to ensure that they were not armed with weapons and let them in. Vladimir was sitting on a throne like chair with a leopard tied next to him. He was feeding it with red meat when they arrived.

He told them, "Sit down. Show your precious five-kilogram Ethiopian opal."

Alamayu said, "I can show you only it's picture on my mobile and will deliver it to you once you give us the cash we deserve."

Vladimir got angry and his tone changed.

He shouted at them, "How dare you two Ethiopians try to negotiate with me? I am the leader of the Russian mafia. With my single gesture I can get you both beheaded."

The Nigerian Ekong intervened and apologized for the Ethiopians and pleaded for his forgiveness, "Alamayu and Mangestu were from out of town and weren't aware of how business is conducted here."

Vladimir didn't listen to Ekong.

He told his men, "Imprison these two and beat the truth about the Opal's location from them."

When the Russian mafia tried to imprison them, they got into a dreadful fist fight. Africans were only three in number but were very strong and huge compared to the Russians. Russians somehow immobilized and captured Alamayu while Mangestu and Ekong fought their way out of there luckily on time and escaped.

Ekong took Mangestu to his old hideout in Goa which only he knew. He told Mangestu to stay low for a while till he figures out a way to free Alamayu.

Mangestu was totally shaken from the incident and asked Ekong with fear, "What will we do if they kill Alamayu?"

Ekong told him, "Don't worry. Vladimir is after the Ethiopian Opal and won't kill Alamayu till he gets it in his custody."

Alamayu was getting badly thrashed by the Russian mafia where they imprisoned him. But Alamayu kept mum and didn't utter a word about the opal's location.

Ekong asked Mangestu, "By the way, do you know where Alamayu had kept the Opal?"

Mangestu said, "Alamayu didn't disclose the Opal's location to me as I am not good at keeping secrets."

Ekong said, "It's okay, I have a plan. You just keep quiet and I will do all the talking with Vladimir."

He called Vladimir and said, "He is ready for the deal and it would be done as per Vladimir's instructions."

Next day, Ekong went with Mangestu again to the secluded mansion of Vladimir. He and Mangestu humbly bowed down to the mafia boss. Ekong took out a pouch from his pocket, opened it, and gave the Opal to Vladimir. He was happy to own an opal.

Vladimir said, "Since I am in a good mood, I will release your Ethiopian friend and let you all go free but forget about the money. Never come back here if you value your lives."

CHAPTER SIX

ALAMAYU AND MANGESTU IN EKONG'S HIDEOUT

After reaching Ekong's hideout in Goa, Alamayu and Mangestu asked Ekong, "Where from you got the Opal?"

Ekong with a cunning smile said, "It is a fake Opal which I gave Vladimir and by the time he realizes that he has been fooled, we will be safe in Bangalore. But you both should avoid going to the paying guest house in Bangalore. I will let you stay in my safe hideout in Bangalore."

Another Nigerian had come to pick them up. They got in the car. Ekong guided the route to his Nigerian friend in their mother tongue Hausa. They reached safely to the hideout without anyone noticing them. Ekong showed them their rooms in the hideout house. He pointed to a fridge and oven in the corner.

He told them, "There is plenty of food supply in the fridge. You just have to heat it in the oven to eat. If you feel so, you can cook something on the stove in the kitchen."

Ekong continued, "I have some urgent matter to take care of. So, I will see you later."

He went out with his Nigerian friend.

Mangestu asked Alamayu, "What if the Russian mafia attacks their previous paying guest house and find the opal there?"

Alamayu said, "Don't worry! I have hidden the Opal at a safe place somewhere else."

Mangestu requested him a lot to tell about the whereabouts of the Opal.

Alamayu finally told him, "I kept it hidden and locked in my locker at Ramaiah Engineering College."

The Russian mafia reached their old paying guest house. They held the house owner at gunpoint and searched the whole house but they couldn't find the Opal. In anger, they broke everything in the house. They beat the house owner badly and asked him the location of the two absconding Ethiopians.

The house owner said, "They were missing for a while and would certainly let you know when they get back."

The Russians gave him their number to call if the Ethiopians contact him, and left. The house owner immediately called Alamayu and told him about the Russians.

Alamayu told him, "I cannot disclose my whereabouts at present. I will get back to you later, once everything had settled down."

Alamayu heated the chicken biriyani from fridge, in the oven. They had Indian chicken biriyani for the first time. They found it mouthwatering but very spicy. Mangestu found a beer bottle in the fridge and got to drinking. Alamayu had a few drinks but Mangestu was a heavy drinker and kept on drinking till he was wasted. They were finding it boring to spend days in Ekong's hideout. Mangestu was feeling very lonely. He spotted from the window a Bangalore kid was walking with a bat and ball.

Mangestu called him and asked, "Are you playing basketball?"

The kid replied, "No, in India we are big fans of cricket. But you are more than welcome to join us to play cricket."

Mangestu and Alamayu went to try playing cricket. They were given a small briefing of how to play cricket by the kids. At first, Alamayu and Mangestu were getting out on first ball itself. Mangestu soon picked up the game and started hitting only sixers with the bat, which surprised the kids. Alamayu discovered that he had a nag for spin balling and was making the kids out on his subsequent spin balls. When the match got over, they thanked the kids for including them in their cricket match.

Alamayu and Mangestu felt tired after the match. Ekong was waiting for them sitting on a couch in their room. He scolded them badly.

He almost screamed, "What the hell are you doing? This house is supposed to be your hideout. But you both were playing cricket out in the open meant risking your lives along with mine."

He warned them, "Stay put in the house till the Russian mafia situation cools down."

They listened to him and kept themselves confined to the house and spend their time watching Tv-shows and news channels. Mangestu again started drinking beer as usual. They were staying hidden in the east of Bangalore at Kammanahalli.

Many Nigerians used to reside in East Bangalore and operated their drug business from there. Because of

Nigerian drug cartels, Bangalore was called the drug capital of India. Ekong, as usual, came at night to meet them.

Mangestu, out of curiosity, asked him, "How Nigerians are operating their drug cartel in Bangalore?"

Ekong said, "The Nigerian drug peddlers are exporting drugs through couriers who are unaware that they are carrying drugs. Nigerian drug sellers also came as overseas students in Bangalore."

Ekong further revealed, "Most Nigerians came on student visa. They overstayed indulging in drug peddling, prostitution and sending spam mails. The Bangalore people never bothered to check the validity of their visas and rented their apartments to these drug peddlers.

Alamayu asked, "Where do they stay?"

"Most of them are staying at Kamanahalli, East Bangalore. Some policemen are also on their payroll. They rescued them from being deported. Nigerian drug peddlers mainly targeted the youth as they were easy to be brainwashed and become their prey." Ekong said.

He continued, "Nigerian cartel mostly dealt with ganja, cannabis, marijuana and weed. They sold it in known circles only. They brought this drug consignment through goods trains and they unlocked it at railway stations like Yashwanthpur cantonments were parcels are not checked."

Mangestu became curious, "How did they flourish here?"

"Nigerian drug mafia flourished in the silicon city due to the affluent overworked professionals, fun seeking students and youngsters who wanted to get high on drugs, especially on the weekends. Students were given free samples initially. Later on, they become addicts, by a mere usage of three or four doses. Some students will gradually turn to drug peddlers to raise money to fulfill their addiction.

Apart from Kamanahalli, in Banaswadi also many Nigerians stayed." Ekong answered.

Ekong told them, "I have good news for you. My Nigerian mafia boss had taken interest in your Ethiopian Opal and would like to buy it."

Alamayu said, "Fine! We just want to sell the opal somehow and don't really care who the buyer is."

Ekong said, "Good for you."

He took Alamayu and Mangestu to their Nigerian boss Abegunde.

He invited the Ethiopians in his house, "Welcome, welcome, Men of Abyssinia."

Abyssinia was the initial name of the Ethiopian country.

He again greeted them, "Come, my fellow Africans. Make yourself at home and take your seats. I have heard the Ethiopian Opal brings immense fortune and luck to whoever possess it and I think that you two Ethiopians have become lucky to meet me."

Mangestu and Alamayu were overwhelmed with joy.

"I will make you an offer. I can give you one million for the Ethiopian Opal but either in black money or one million worth drug merchandise. Now the ball is in your court. Take your time and think over it. You can tell Ekong when you are ready to make the deal. He is my second in command and will lead you both right to me. 'Ciao' for now my fellow Ethiopians. See you soon." He said.

After reaching their hideout, Alamayu and Mangestu told Ekong, "We neither want black money nor drugs merchandise. We want white money in cash and that too two million which is the right price of the Ethiopian Opal."

Ekong said, "Alright! Chill down. I will soon find out somebody in Bangalore who could pay around two million for the opal. Just have faith in me and don't go out in the open as the Russian mafia is searching for you everywhere."

Mangestu soon got bored of sitting in the room. He kept looking outside his room window at whoever was passing on the road.

CHAPTER SEVEN

MANGESTU MEETS DONNA

One day, while gazing through the window, he saw a beautiful Bangalore girl walking on the road with her handbag. She was quite fair, had silky hair and well-toned body. She was wearing a blue top, black skirt and had a golden chain on her neck. A guy with handkerchief covered on his face was following her. He snatched the golden chain on her neck and started running. Mangestu couldn't stand this. He came down the room, ran after the robber. He got hold of his collar from behind, pinned him down and beat the crap out of him. He got the girl's golden chain and returned her the same. She thanked him from the bottom of her heart.

Mangestu asked her, "Your good name please."

She replied, "Donna."

"How come you are walking alone on the road?" He asked.

The girl replied, "I was returning home after my engineering classes."

"But you should have been careful." Ekong said.

She said with surprise, "You don't look Indian. Where exactly are you from?"

Mangestu said, "I am an Ethiopian, from Addis Ababa. Here on business purpose, staying two blocks ahead."

Donna asked "Where is this Addia Ababa?"

Mangestu said, "in the year 1999, Adv. Smita Sivadasan, a poetess and novelist visited Addis Ababa. Her first impression of Addis Ababa came out in the form of a poetry, which was published in 'The Monitor,' the leading daily of Addis Ababa," and he cited the poem.

"OH! ADDIS!

Oh! Addis! I adore you.
Away, away, in India, I wondered
"Where is Addis Ababa?"
I turned the globe round and round
You were not to be seen.
I stooped and stooped hours and hours
Over the largest world's map.
You were not to be seen.
My vain strain to trace you lingered on....
I got you, at last, hiding
In the 'water-tower' of eastern Africa.
Oh! Elegant, lovely highland resort!
I stepped in your amicable lap
Stand gaping, bewitched
Witnessing your arresting Beauty.
Oh! The land of moors and mountains!
You dwell so high stretching
To snuggle the Heaven above.
Your sweet-smelling roses cast
Alluring aroma around.
Red and purple bracts of your bougainvillea
Make dainty dance in the air.

49

How I love the smell of roasted coffee seeds
Emanates from your balmy breeze!
Oh! Mother Nature's dearest child!
You ramble so gracefully across the wooded hillside.
Oh! The land of flora and fauna!
Your falcon, kestrel and verreaux's eagle
Hovers high and high above.
Your entrancing rivers and lakes flow
Elegantly throwing life out of gear.
Your serene afternoon breeze whisper in my ears
"Behold! Behold! Addis is a delightful place to live."
Oh! The land of cadence and music!
When the golden beams of sun
Play hide and seek abaft your hilltop
Whilst the whole galaxy of the wide firmament
Descends below and scintillate on your tree tops,
While the glimmering half – moon
Flits in and out of the dark clouds
Your gentle evening breeze soothe my aching soul
And assuage the anguish of exiting my homeland;
The sweet aroma of your garden plants
Drugs me to some unknown ecstasy.
Slowly and slowly, I resign to an extreme rapture.
Safe, Safe, in your amiable lap, I wonder
"Where am I"
Eureka! I am in my lost paradise.
Oh! Bountiful Mother Nature
Bless my Addis to soar and soar
Above the blue unknown for ever and ever."
[Courtsey – Adv. Smita Sivadasan]
She exclaimed, "What a lovely depiction of Addis Ababa!"

Mangestu said, "Yes, it's a beautiful poem. The true feelings of an Indian poetess."

She remarked, "Wow! Eventhough you are not from my country, you had the heart to help me out. You seem a nice guy."

Mangestu said, "I am just your friendly neighbor," and asked her, "By the way, what engineering course do you study?"

She said, "I am doing B. tech in Metallurgy."

Mangestu told her, "My friend Alamayu has also done B. tech in Metallurgy. If you have any doubts, you can come to our house. I will tell him to clear all your doubts."

She said, "Thanks, I will get in touch with you."

The very next day, Donna came to Mangestu's house and knocked his door.

Mangestu opened the door and said, "What a pleasant surprise! What brings such a beautiful girl to my door step?"

She blushed and said, "I had a few doubts in Metallurgy and would your friend be kind enough to clear my doubts?"

Mangestu said, "Sure. Take your seat, I will tell him right away to clear your doubts."

He went inside the room, brought Alamayu and introduced Donna to him.

Mangestu told Donna, "Alamayu is a genius in Metallurgy and will make you a master in Metallurgy likewise."

Donna asked Alamayu a few doubts in Metallurgy. Though Alamayu was explaining Metallurgy in depth to her, Donna kept ogling Mangestu. After Alamayu finished explaining her, Mangestu came to see her off.

She asked him, "What are you doing on the weekend?"

He said, "Nothing special."

Donna said, "Then, we would go for sight-seeing on the weekend. I will show you around in Bangalore. It's the least I can do to return you the favor of saving my golden chain from that robber."

Mangestu said, "Fine! I will see you in the weekend then."

Donna said, "Ciao!" and went happily.

On the weekend, Donna took Mangestu on her bike to Shivajinagar. There they went to checkout St. Mary's Basilica church. People come from around the world to visit this church. This is the only church in Karnataka which has the status of Basilica. The magnificent pillars and stained-glass windows of the church were imported from Belgium. The church has statues of various Saints. Among them, the statue of patron Saint is believed to have miraculous powers. Mangestu and Donna prayed for a while there. Mangestu prayed that someone rich should soon approach him and Alamayu to buy the Ethiopian Opal.

Thereafter, Donna took him to the Pyramid Valley in Bangalore located at thirty kilometers from the center of Bangalore city.

Donna told Mangestu, "This Buddha pyramid is the biggest meditation pyramid in the world. Its design was inspired by the great pyramid of Giza. It could accommodate about five thousand visitors at a time. Its base is made of cement and body is built of steel. The steel frame is positioned in such a way to manifest the four main elements - air, water, fire and earth. The south signifies fire, the north signifies air, the east signifies water and the west signifies earth. The space within the big pyramid signifies the fifth element which is ether."

Mangestu was a good listener.

Donna said, "People mostly come here to do yoga and meditation."

She asked him, "Would you like to meditate here?"

Mangestu said, "I have a better idea."

He got down on his knees and proposed her.

He said, "I have fallen in love with you. I want to marry you."

Donna blushed and said, "Yes me too," and agreed to marry him.

Then they took a lot of their romantic pictures there and had food together which the management of the pyramid valley served totally free of cost.

Mangestu asked Donna, "Where to next?"

She said, "Now, we will visit the largest bull in Bangalore."

Mangestu was confused.

She laughed, "Don't worry Mangestu, I am taking you to a very old temple of bull in Bangalore."

Mangestu heaved a sigh of relief. After reaching Basavanagudi, she took him to the bull temple and showed him the huge statue of the bull. This humungous bull temple was constructed by Kempe Gowda in Dravidian style. It's one of the oldest Nandi temples in the country. It was carved out of a single granite rock.

Mangestu said, "I am exhausted. Shall we continue our sight-seeing tomorrow?"

Donna said, "Okay, by all means".

She dropped him on her bike back to his residence.

On reaching home, Alamayu shouted at Mangestu, "Have you lost your senses, man? Going out in broad daylight with a localite, you are risking our exposure to the Russian mafia."

Mangestu was cool. He said, "Chill man! The Russian mafia has no clue where we are. I have fallen in love with the Bangalore girl Donna. I will protect her with my life if needed."

Alamayu said, "Alright! Just be careful not to come in the vicinity of the Russian mafia."

On Sunday, Donna took Mangestu to Lalabagh Botanical Garden. Mangestu was astonished to see the Lalbagh glass house in the Botanical garden. He enjoyed viewing the flora and fauna there.

Donna told him, "Its construction was started by Hyder Ali but was completed by his son Tipu Sultan."

Mangestu interrupted, "Wait, wait, by the way, who is this Hyder Ali?"

Donna said, "He was a 'defacto' Muslim ruler of Mysore. He was also the military commander."

Mangestu said, "Okay, continue."

"Hyder Ali wanted to make the Lalbag botanical garden resemble The Mughal Gardens. Tipu Sultan imported a lot of trees and plants from various countries. Lalbagh is around two hundred forty acres garden and accommodates more than thousand species of plants with many trees that are more than hundred years old. There were also some rare species of plants brought from Persia, Afghanistan and France." She continued.

Mangestu said, "This is a marvelous Botanical Garden that I had ever seen."

Donna also showed him the Lalbagh Rock.

She explained, "This is the most ancient form of rock on earth. It is about three thousand million years old."

Mangestu was surprised by her knowledge in history and said, "You should become a historian rather than becoming an engineer, as your wide knowledge in history can fetch you a lot of money."

Donna laughed and they both started returning home on her bike, when all of a sudden, they were surrounded by Russian mafia cars. When Mangestu got down the bike to tackle them, he was hit with a rod on his head from behind. Mangestu fell unconscious. They used chloroform to make Donna unconscious and kidnapped her. After some time, when Mangestu regained his conscious, he noted his head was bleeding and Donna was nowhere to be seen. He got in a taxi and quickly reached his hideout at Kamanahalli. After paying the taxi driver off, he told Alamayu about the unfortunate events that unfolded that day.

Alamayu said, "I warned you many times to be careful but you, moron, you just didn't listen. Let me call Ekong, He may know how to trace Donna."

Ekong reached there soon and he was shocked on hearing what had happened.

Ekong said, "Quick, pack everything. We need to leave this city as soon as possible."

Mangestu said, "Not without Donna. Donna the cute Bangalore girl, is the love of my life and I am not going anywhere without finding her first."

Ekong said, "I told you guys to stay low for a while but instead you involved a Bangalore girl in the middle of this mess. Let me call my friends in the Nigerian mafia and try to locate the girl."

Within an hour, he traced the location of the Russian mafia where they were holding Donna imprisoned.

Ekong said, "They are hiding her at their real estate front in Bangalore."

He further said, "With my fellow Nigerian gang members, I can rescue her. In order to do so, I now want fifty per cent of the share money you would get by selling the Ethiopian Opal."

Alamayu said, "Fine! You greedy bastard! Somehow get Mangestu's girlfriend back in one piece."

Ekong smiled cunningly and went to meet his fellow Nigerian gang members. They got ready with heavy artillery to attack the Russian mafia. They had kept Donna tied in their go- down. Ekong and his men surrounded the go-down and started firing at them. The firing continued for a long while. There were casualties on both sides of the mafia gangs. Ekong threw a non-lethal tear gas grenade at them which blinded them temporarily. Using this situation to his advantage, he got into the go-down wearing a gas mask without anybody noticing him, and told Donna that he had come on Mangestu's behalf to save her. He untied Donna and cleverly rescued her from there. Ekong brought Donna safely to their hideout in Kamanahalli.

Mangestu was happy to see her again and hugged her with joy.

Mangestu asked Donna, "Should I accompany you?"
She said, "Sure."

Mangestu asked Donna about her parents and if she had any siblings.

Donna replied, "I have a younger sister studying economics at a nearby college. My father is a politician and my Mom is a homemaker."

Mangestu said, "Wow! your Dad is a politician! That means your family must be very influential."

She said, "Yes, a kind of. My Dad is contesting for the post of MLA in the upcoming elections."

When they almost reached her house, Mangestu asked, "Can I take you out tomorrow for a movie?"

She nodded her head in acceptance.

Mangestu said, "Nice! I shall come to pick you tomorrow sharp at 4:00 PM."

She smiled and said, "Looking forward to it."

Mangestu told Alamayu about his plan to take Donna out for a movie and about her family.

Alamayu became furious. He shouted at the top of his voice, "You stupid! You won't listen to me. Do whatever you want."

Mangestu replied, "Anything for the sake of love."

After sometime, Alamayu cautioned, "Be careful Mangestu. Make sure that you don't offend her Dad in any manner. Being a politician, with his influence, he could get us deported to Ethiopia if he wants to harm us."

Mangestu said, "Chill bro! I am very pleasing and everyone likes me. It won't be a problem."

Mangestu came to pick Donna for the movie at sharp 4:00 PM. He knocked at her door. To his surprise, she opened the door in an elegant red top and skirt. She was looking totally gorgeous and was a feast for the eyes. Her politician father came to see them off. At first he thanked Mangestu for saving his daughter's life from a burglar and for returning her golden chain.

Mangestu said, "You are welcome, sir. I just helped her out, as it's the duty of any friendly neighbor to do so."

Her father said, "Alright gentleman! I hope you will take good care of my daughter and bring her back home safe by dinner time."

Mangestu said, "Sure sir."

He went with Donna for the movie.

He took Donna to PVR, a theatre which was very famous in Bangalore for the luxury and comfort the theatre provided. He got two corner seat tickets for them for a romantic movie. The seating was sofa like. They sat close to each other holding hand in hand. During interval time, Mangestu brought Donna diet coke and pizza. While some steamy scenes were going on in the cinema, they couldn't control themselves and gave each other hugs and kisses. Mangestu brought Donna back home safe and sound, as promised.

Her father invited Mangestu for dinner, "Why can't you have dinner with us, young man?"

He humbly denied, "Some other time, Sir, my friend Alamayu might be waiting for me to have dinner."

Mangestu came to his room filled with joy. Almayu was waiting for him for dinner.

While having dinner Alamayu asked, "How is Donna's father?"

Mangestu said, "He is quite friendly as a politician is supposed to get along with everybody. Her father will definitely make to the MLA post in the upcoming elections."

He added, "Though her father looked frightening with his thick moustache, beard and huge size, he is quite down to earth."

CHAPTER EIGHT

VLADIMIR AND THE ETHIOPIAN OPAL

Right then, they heard someone knocking their door. Alamayu went to open the door. As he opened the door, he was shocked to see the Russian mafia standing in front of him with guns pointing at them. They barged in their house, tied Alamayu and Mangestu on chairs. The Russian mafia tortured them and beaten them severely to make them speak where they are hiding their Ethiopian Opal, but they kept mum. Mangestu couldn't bear the torture for long and he finally broke and told them the location of the Ethiopian Opal.

The Russian mafia got into Ramaiah College, broke open Alamayu's locker and stole the Ethiopian Opal and brought it to their mafia leader Vladimir. He locked the Opal in a safe upstairs in his bedroom in his huge mansion.

Mangestu apologized to Alamayu, "I didn't have the stamina to withstand any more beating by the Russians. So, I disclosed the location of the Opal to them. Please forgive me."

Alamayu said, "It's okay, Mangestu, I understand, don't worry. We just have to wait for Ekong to reach us."

After a couple of hours, Ekong came to their residence and was startled to see them tied on chairs. He untied them and asked them what had happened. Alamayu told Ekong how they were attacked by the Russians and tortured till finally Mangestu broke and gave them the Opal's location.

Ekong cried in despair, "Damn it! By now they might have got their hands on the Ethiopian Opal."

After sometime he said, "Don't lose all hope. I will find a way to relocate the Opal from the Russian mafia's custody. But at first we need to change our hideout as it's compromised to be on the safer side"

Ekong called his fellow Nigerian gang members. They came in a black SUV and took them to their new hideout.

Ekong told Alamayu and Mangestu, "I have ordered my gang members to be on the lookout for the Ethiopian Opal among Russians and give us information if they come around."

He told the Ethiopians, "Settle down here for a while. As soon the Russian mafia would try to seek a buyer for the sale of the Opal, and when they are about to make a deal, that's when we will strike and snatch our Opal from beneath their noses."

He left them some food supply and beer before leaving. Mangestu was disappointed for not being able to withstand the Russians torture, and took to drinking as usual to cope up with his failure. Then Alamayu and Mangestu had some injera and doro wat which Ekong had got them from an Ethiopian Hotel in Bangalore. Mangestu again started drinking and was totally wasted again.

After a few days, Ekong came to meet them and told them, "The Russian mafia had made their move in contacting a buyer for the Opal who is a Bangalore underworld Don called Nagesh. Nagesh being superstitious is ready to pay Vladimir two million dollars for the Ethiopian Opal. He believed the Opal would empower their gang to flourish in Bangalore."

Alamayu asked, "When is the deal?"

Ekong said, "The deal is about to go down at an isolated street corner tomorrow at noon."

He gave them guns and told them, "Get ready to retaliate."

By next day noon, Ekong, Alamayu, Mangestu and the Nigerian gang members were in position with guns at the top of the buildings near the street. Vladimir and his gang arrived on time. Vladimir got out of his car and called Nagesh for the deal. By noon, Nagesh and his gang members came in a series of SUVs.

Nagesh told Vladimir, "Show me the Ethiopian Opal."

Vladimir said, "First show me the two million in cash."

Nagesh said, "Fine"!

He told one of his men to get the suitcase with money from his car. He opened the suitcase and showed him the money. In return, when Vladimir was about to take the Ethiopian Opal from his jacket pocket, Ekong and his men started firing guns at them. Nagesh took the suitcase and quickly got in his car and escaped. The Russian mafia also opened fire at Ekong and his men. Vladimir shot Ekong on his shoulder. The Nigerians responded back by firing fiercely at the Russians. Many Russians were shot dead. When Vladimir saw that he was losing the battle, he soon got in his car with his men and swiftly drove off to safety. Alamayu and Mangestu helped Ekong and reached back to their hideout. Many Nigerians had also lost their lives to the battle.

Alamayu told Mangestu, "Get the first aid kit. Quick. Fast!"

He removed the bullet and bandaged Ekong's shoulder.

Alamayu advised Ekong, "You better take rest. You have lost a lot of blood."

Ekong slept for a while and after he woke up, he told them, "Don't worry, we will definitely get it next time."

Afterwards, when Ekong's shoulder had healed of the gun shot injury, he contacted the Ethiopians and told them, "I got a tip from one of my Nigerian gang members that Vladimir had locked the Opal in a safe in his bedroom upstairs in his mansion."

He added, "One of my men would get the blue print of Vladimir's mansion, using which we could plan an attack on his mansion for retrieving the Ethiopian Opal."

By evening, his men had obtained the blueprint for Ekong. As per the blue print there was a tunnel like drainage that opened behind Vladimir's mansion in his compound.

Ekong told them, "Vladimir's mistress from Russia is coming to meet him and her plane would land this weekend in Bangalore. Security will be to a minimum when Vladimir will be spending quality time with his mistress upstairs in his bedroom and that's precisely when we should strike."

When the weekend approached, Ekong, his men, Alamayu and Mangestu were ready with guns to attack Vladimir's mansion. They waited for nightfall. They drove in a black SUV, parked it right behind the drainage opening site. They got in the drainage tunnel one by one. It was stinking badly inside the tunnel due to the drainage system. They rapidly walked through the tunnel and reached its opening behind Vladimir's mansion in his compound. They opened the drainage tunnel opening, got in quietly without anyone noticing. They got in Vladimir's mansion from the backdoor of the kitchen. They made their way through the kitchen by shooting down the chef and cooks in Vladimir's kitchen. They reached the center of the mansion's ground floor. The Nigerians and Ethiopians shot down Vladimir's guards from behind quietly, as they used silencer for their guns. Cautiously they climbed the staircase to Vladimir's bedroom. As they had expected, the upper floor was not so heavily guarded. They shot down his few guards upstairs.

Ekong kicked open Vladimir's bedroom door. Vladimir and his mistress were having Vodka on a sofa and were bewildered by the Nigerians and Ethiopians forceful entry in his bedroom. Alaamyu pointed gun at Vladimir and told Ekong to open the safe. When Ekong tried a combination of digits on the safe to open it, the alarm went on. Vladimir had cunningly fitted an alarm to the safe which alerted the nearby police station. Alamayu, Mangestu, Ekong and his men, within a fraction of a second, climbed down the stairs and escaped through the drainage tunnel, before the police reached the mansion. They got in their SUVs and escaped but their planned attempt had gone south.

After reaching their hideout, Ekong said, "We need someone who is an expert in cracking the safe open without the alarm switching on."

Ekong sent his men in order to find out an expert in safe cracking. In due course of time, one of his guys informed of a localite by name Manjunath who had just got out of prison for robbing the safe of a wealthy businessman.

Ekong said, "Good work! He is perfect for our job. Where can I find him?"

The guy on Ekong's payroll said, "He can be seen getting wasted drinking every night at the local bar downtown."

Ekong went to meet him with his men at the bar, where his guy showed Manjunath drinking heavily at a corner table. Ekong offered him a few drinks.

Manjunath gladly accepted the drinks and asked him, "To what I owed this pleasure?"

Ekong introduced himself and told him, "I have a job for you which require your expertise in cracking safes."

Manjunath said, "Only if you agree to pay me ten percent of whatever you intend to get from the safe."

Ekong agreed to pay him ten percent of the Opal sale money by saying, "Man, you Bangaloreans drive a hard bargain."

Ekong told the Ethiopians "I got a safe cracking expert on my side, so get ready to carry out the heist."

"But this time, we need to proceed with extra caution as Vladimir might have tightened his security upstairs near the safe." He added.

Ekong told Alamayu and Mangestu, "Vladimir is planning to host a party this coming fortnight where all the big shots of Bangalore will be present including politicians and policemen on his payroll. We could get in disguised as men from the catering company booked for the party."

Ekong got his Nigerian men, Manjunath and the Ethiopians, catering dress uniform of the catering company. The night of the party, they arrived on time of the buffet to begin. They got into the mansion unnoticed, dressed in caterers' uniforms. They had brought their weapons concealed in the food containers. As soon as they climbed upstairs, they took out their guns from the food containers, shot at the guards upstairs. To their surprise, the guards had bullet proof vests on them. Without getting hurt, they shot back at them. Most of Ekong's men were getting shot dead. Somehow Ekong, giving cover to

Manjunath, got him near the safe. He destroyed the safety alarm. When he was just about to crack open the safe, one of the guards shot Manjunath on his forehead. Alamayu saw Vladimir's mistress at a distance. Quickly he nabbed her and pointed his gun at her forehead.

Alamayu threatened, "If you want your mistress alive, give us safe passage out of the mansion."

Being helpless, Vladimir allowed them out of the mansion. They took his mistress hostage in their SUV and warned them not to follow or else they would shoot her dead. When they reached halfway, they threw Vladimir's mistress out of the SUV next to a pavement and drove to their hideout. Vladimir's men brought his mistress back safely but he was greatly offended by the Africans attempt for retrieving the Ethiopian Opal. Once again, the Ethiopians were back to square one. Their attempt had gone sideways. Alamayu and Mangestu drank alcohol in utter disappointment and grief.

It was a sunny afternoon when Mangestu got a call from Donna.

She cried, "My sister was kidnapped on her way back from college. The kidnappers had called my Dad and were demanding fifty lakh rupees as ransom money for her safe return to us."

Mangestu said, "Calm down Donna, we will figure out something. But does your Dad have that kind of money?"

Donna replied, "Yes, like other corrupt politicians, my dad also had lot of black money stashed in his account in Swiss bank. I have been requesting Dad to get out of this dirty politics but he just won't listen. He kept on saying that all this money is for our bright future."

Mangestu asked, "Your father had informed the police?"

Donna said, "No, the kidnapers had strictly warned against doing so. They threatened my Dad that he would find my sister's dead body somewhere in the gutter if he informs the police."

Mangestu said, "Don't worry, Donna, I will try to find out the kidnappers through my Nigerian friends. Everything will be all right; God will protect your sister. I will pray for her safety."

Donna said, "Thanks, I will let you know when the kidnappers contact us again."

Mangestu told Alamayu about Donna's sister's kidnapping.

Alamayu said, "Man, let them deal with it. They are localites, we shouldn't interfere in their matter. Remember this is a hideout, we are supposed to stay under the radar of the Russian mafia. I just heard that Vladimir has declared one million cash prize to contract killers whoever beheads us first."

Mangestu insisted by saying, "Alamayu, she is the love of my life, I can't imagine life without her."

Alamayu finally agreed and called Ekong for his help.

Ekong said, "I will do the needful. I will try to find the kidnappers soon."

Ekong soon found where they were holding Donna's sister captive. It was a garage which had been closed for a while.

Ekong said, "Let's free her quickly before they shift her elsewhere."

Donna called Mangestu and told him that the kidnappers had contacted them to deliver the ransom money before sunset for which her father had to go alone.

Mangestu said, "Tell your father to continue as planned. We will let you know when we free your sister as we have located where she is held captive."

Donna said, "Thanks, please be careful."

Mangestu, Alamayu, Ekong and his Nigerian men had surrounded the garage. Ekong kicked open the garage door. They shot the kidnappers before they had any chance of pointing their gun at them. Mangestu found Donna's sister horrified and tied at a corner.

Mangestu said, "I am Donna's friend" and untied her.

He called Donna's father and conveyed, "We had rescued your daughter. So, no need to pay any ransom money."

Mangestu brought Donna's sister back home safe in one piece. Her family was happy to see her alive. Donna thanked Mangestu from the bottom of her heart.

Mangestu said, "No need to thank me, anything for you dear."

When Donna's family was getting back to normal, Donna's sister started experiencing seizures off and on. They took her to a Doctor. The Doctor said she was getting seizures because of the terrifying experience she had in the captivity of the kidnappers and also that she had gone into a state of severe depression. He referred her to a psychiatrist who prescribed her pills for controlling her seizures and depression. But, day by day, Donna's sister's condition was worsening. She denied eating or drinking anything and confined herself to her bed for days together. Her parents were getting worried. They contacted a psychologist who agreed to come to their house and start cognitive behavior therapy to help their daughter.

He said, "She needs at least three to six months of therapy sessions to fully recover."

Her parents agreed to his methods. The psychologist charged heavily every time he came for the sessions.

Though six months of the therapy sessions were over, yet there was no improvement in her condition. Cognitive behavior therapy was all in vain. Mangestu felt pity on Donna's sister's condition and told Alamayu her condition.

He told Alamayu, "Her state could be reversed with the help of Opal's medicinal properties if only we can get our hands on it."

He convinced Alamayu for a very small piece of Opal as talisman for Donna's sister to cure her of her seizure and depression when they would succeed in retrieving the Opal from Vladimir's custody. Right then Ekong came to meet them.

He said, "I have a new plan for extracting the Opal from Vladimir. I came to know about Vladimir's daughter Natasha who is here to meet Vladimir from Russia. She is very much fond of sun basking at the beach and partying all night long. Apparently she is hanging out at Gokarna beach near Bangalore."

Ekong added, "I will befriend her at the beach, find out her weakness and then we can capture her. That way we will have leverage over Vladimir. I am sure, in exchange for his beloved daughter's life, he will surely give us back our rightful Ethiopian Opal."

At around noon, when Natasha was sun basking at the beach, Ekong came and sat right next to her.

He said 'Hi' to Natasha and introduced himself to her as a tourist visiting India.

He asked, "What made a beautiful damsel like you to come to India?"

Natasha said, "I am on vacation and what better way to enjoy one's vacation than by sun basking, booze and doing drugs."

Ekong and Natasha had a laugh on that note. Ekong asked her out for a party at the beach that night.

She said, "Yes, by all means, that's why I am here to rock the party."

It was a glamorous party with foreign tourists pouring in from all over to chill in the party. Ekong asked Natasha for a dance.

After dancing for a while Natasha said, "I am finding the party a kind of boring."

"I wanna get high on drugs. Do you know where I can get some good quality cocaine to get high?" She asked.

Ekong said, "For sure, I know a few drug dealers. Come with me. It's time to get high."

Ekong took Natasha away from the party to an isolated place of the beach where Alamayu and Mangestu where sitting at the back of a van waiting for them to arrive.

Ekong said, "The dealer is in the van, come on, let's get into the van."

Alamayu took her by surprise, made her unconscious with a handkerchief dipped in a bit of chloroform. She laid unconscious in the van. Ekong quickly drove the van to their secret hideout. When Natasha regained her conscious, she found herself immobilized, tied on a sofa. Ekong, Mangestu and Alamayu were sitting on a sofa opposite to her.

Ekong said, "Good morning Mademoiselle, you had been unconscious for a while, you had us worrying because you are of no use to us dead."

Natasha spit on Ekong and said, "You don't know who you are messing with. My Dad is the Russian mafia boss. He will get you all slaughtered if you don't let me go."

Ekong laughed at her and made a call to Vladimir.

He said, "Hello Vladimir, your lovely daughter is in our captivity. If you want her back alive, you better return us our Ethiopian Opal, which is rightfully ours and don't try playing any tricks if you are bothered about your daughter's safety."

Vladimir said, "Fine! Give me some time. I will get you the Opal."

Ekong said, "You have till noon tomorrow. I have messaged you the address. If you don't get us the Opal by tomorrow noon, you can forget about your daughter."

Vladimir called up a police officer named Daniel on his payroll who was known for carrying out numerous encounters in the city. He offered him one million to kill the Africans and to get back his daughter safe and sound from their captivity.

Vladimir said, "The money will be transferred to your account as soon as you get me back my daughter alive. I believe killing the Africans won't be a problem for you as you are an encounter specialist."

The police officer said, "Consider it done, and message me their location."

Daniel informed his police station that he had got a tip regarding a drugs deal happening at the location where the Africans were holding Natasha captive. Daniel got his policemen ready for making a raid for the drugs. He attacked Ekong's hideout with a bunch of policemen. The police broke open the door, got in and held the Africans at gunpoint. Alamayu, Mangestu and Ekong were arrested on charges of kidnapping and drug trafficking as Daniel had secretly placed some drugs in Ekong's hideout during the raid there, which the other policemen found later and took it as evidence against the Africans. Daniel freed Natasha and brought her safe back to Vladimir.

Vladimir thanked Daniel and asked him, "The Africans are dead?"

Daniel responded, "Don't worry, I plan on killing them in jail and I will make it look like they were shot dead while trying to escape during the interrogation of their drug cartel whereabouts."

Vladimir said, "Alright! I will wire transfer the money in your account."

Ekong sadly said to the Ethiopians, "I had heard about Daniel the Encounter specialist. I suspect he plans to do our encounter in jail itself."

Ekong further said, "Mangestu, you contact Donna and tell her politician Dad to use his influence in getting us out, before we get killed."

Mangestu requested the constable next to his cell to make a phone call. The constable felt sympathy for the Africans and allowed Mangestu to make a call. Mangestu dialed Donna's number and told her about their dreadful situation in jail and asked for her father's help to get them out. On Donna's request her politician father used his influence, made some calls to higher authorities and told them that it was a misunderstanding regarding the Africans. He said that the Africans were mere innocent foreign students in India who had come for higher studies in India and they had nothing to do with any drug cartel. Daniel had falsely placed drug evidence against them. Donna's father insisted that action should be taken against Daniel and the Africans should be released at once. Due to Donna's father's influence, inspector Daniel was suspended and the Africans were free to go. Vladimir planned to export the Ethiopian Opal to the United States of America and sell it there as Ethiopian Opal was in high demand there for its miraculous properties. He took out the Opal from his safe, placed it in a suitcase with a lock. Handed it over to his trusted Russian men and gave them orders for the Opal to be exported in a cargo ship to the Unites States with tight security. Ekong came to know about the shipment of Opal from his fellow Nigerian informers that it would sail through the Pacific Ocean to reach the U.S.

ETHIOPIANS RETRIEVE THEIR OPAL

Ekong, Alamayu and Mangestu geared up to capture the Opal from the cargo ship on sea. When the cargo ship started to sail and covered some distance on sea, the Africans caught up to the ship in a motor boat. With the help of ropes, they climbed the ship. They opened fire at the guards holding Opal in a suitcase in their custody. Ekong broke open the lock of the suitcase and found their precious Ethiopian Opal. Before they could vanish with the opal, the ship was on attack by the sea pirates. They shot cannon balls from their pirate ship. They overpowered the security personnel on the cargo ship with guns and swords. They stole whatever was valuable in the ship. The pirate captain's eyes caught a glimpse of the Ethiopian Opal in Ekong's hands. As he knew, how precious the Opal was, he confiscated the Opal from the Africans and held them captive in their pirate ship. The captain set for sale across the Pacific Ocean in search for other ships to attack and rob. The Africans were imprisoned in a cellar below the dock of the ship. The pirate captain kept the Ethiopian opal right next to him in his chamber in the ship. After sunset, the pirates addicted to rum, were heavily drinking. By night they were all in deep sleep.

Ekong told the Africans in the cell, "Be alert as now is the ideal time to break out from the cell, as all the pirates are asleep. I know how to pick a lock."

Ekong carefully picked the prison lock with a knife, he kept hidden in his boots, in pin drop silence. They cautiously stole the pirates' guns without waking them up. They got into the captain's room; the pirate captain was also in deep sleep. The Ethiopian Opal was lying next on a table there. Alamayu grabbed the opal. Ekong found some dynamites in the capatain's room. He lit the dynamites after attaching them at every nook and corner of the pirate ship. They quickly jumped off the ship into the sea and started swimming as far as they could. The pirate ship blew into pieces with the explosion of the dynamites. They kept swimming but were getting exhausted. To their luck, they saw a fisherman boat sailing a bit ahead in the sea. They waved at the fisherman for help. The fisherman rowed his boat close to them and brought them on board of the boat to safety. They were all shivering with cold from swimming in the sea. The fisherman gave them some blankets and some alcohol to generate some heat in them. As they reached a sea shore, they were ambushed by Vladimir's men. They got into a brutal fight. The fisherman rapidly sailed away from them to safety as he didn't want to die in vain by unnecessarily getting in between their feud.

The Russians succeeded in defeating the Africans and snatched the Ethiopian Opal from Alamayu's hands. Once again, the ball was in their court as Vladimir's men had regained the Opal from the Africans' possession.

Now, the Ethiopians were staying at Ekong's place as their last hideout was also compromised.

Ekong advised them, "Stay low for a while. Wait for the right opportunity to strike back at the Russians."

After a few months, Ekong heard a rumor about Vladimir trying to make a deal for the Opal with a Dubai Sheikh for two million dollars. He confirmed from his Nigerian men in the underworld that the rumor is right. He told Alamayu and Mangestu about the Dubai Sheikh coming to India to buy the Ethiopian Opal.

Ekong said, "Fate is on our side, we have yet another chance to get the opal."

He found out the time of arrival of the Sheikh's flight from his men.

He told Alamayu and Mangestu, "The Sheikh is arriving via Emirates airline at 6:00 PM tomorrow. We need to figure out a way so that the Sheikh cooperates with us at the airport terminal."

Ekong and his men acted as Vladimir's men and got to the Sheikh at the airport terminal before Vladimir's men reached by holding a placard with the Sheikh's name on it. They took him to an SUV outside the airport under the impression of taking him to Vladimir's mansion. Instead, they brought him to Ekong's place and imprisoned him there. They dressed up Alamayu as the Dubai Sheikh with long beard and made him wear loose white robe, a scarf on his head with a strong cord to hold it in place. Ekong and his men acted as his hired muscle with fake moustache and beard. They went to Vladimir's mansion to make the deal. The guards at the entrance stopped them from entering the mansion.

Alamayu said, "Tell your boss Vladimir that the Sheikh has come for making the deal."

One of the guards went inside, sought Vladimir's permission, and then allowed them inside the mansion.

Vladimir said, "I had my men to pick you up but you were nowhere to be seen at the airport terminal."

The Sheikh said, "Let bygones be bygones my friend. Now let's quickly make the deal, and then I have an urgent meeting to attend overseas with my other business partners."

Vladimir said, "Yes, Why not? First show me the Dubai Dirhams equivalent to two million dollars."

Alamayu opened the suitcase and showed him the fake Dirham currency that Ekong had given him to fool Vladimir.

By seeing the suitcase filled with money, Vladimir said, with a smile, "Now you are speaking business, my man. It's not for nothing that Sheikhs are known to keep their word."

Vladimir opened the safe and handed over the Ethiopian Opal to Alamayu in disguise as the Sheikh.

The Sheikh bid farewell to Vladimir by saying, "It was nice doing business with you."

They got in their SUV and made a run for their lives before Vladimir figured out that they had handed over him fake money. Vladimir soon figured out that he was duped by the Africans with fake Dirhams. Vladimir sent his men after the Africans. They chased the SUV in which the Africans were escaping. They fired from behind at the SUV. They shot the SUV's tyres flat. The Africans got out and ran for their lives in all possible directions. But Ekong was shot in the back by the Russians. They captured him and brought Ekong to Vladimir's mansion. They tied him to a chair. Vladimir made his men torture Ekong badly to know the whereabouts of the Opal with the Ethiopians. They beat him with a bat till he bleed and pulled out his teeth.

Ekong cried in agony and told them finally, "I will take you to the exact location of the Ethiopian Opal."

Ekong took Vladimir and his men to his Nigerian boss Abegunde's house. By seeing the Russians, Abegunde and his men pointed their guns at them, as apparently, they were rival gangs. Vladimir commanded Abegunde to return him the Opal.

Abegunde said, "What Opal?" and opened fire at them.

The Russians too started shooting back in response. Ekong carefully hid behind a pillar. The firing between the gangs continued for a while till both the Russian and Nigerian gangs perished in the crossfire. Ekong came out from behind the pillar after the bloodshed was over. He was the only smart one to have remained alive. Ekong, though, was shot in the back, with great difficulty, hired a cab and reached his house where the Ethiopians and his remaining Nigerian men had regrouped. Alamayu and Mangestu helped Ekong and carefully removed the bullet from his back.

When Ekong was revived, they told him, "The Sheikh had died of heart attack right where you had imprisoned him."

As Alamayu already agreed, he allowed Mangestu to give a very small piece of the Opal as talisman to be worn by Donna's sister. In a short span of time, Donna's sister's condition got fully reversed. The Ethiopian Opal cured her of her seizures and depression.

Now that Mangestu had saved Donna's sister's life, her father offered his daughter's hand in marriage to Mangestu. Mangestu wholeheartedly accepted the proposal.

Ekong told Alamayu and Mangestu, "I plan to retire after getting my share of money by selling the Ethiopian Opal."

Ekong added, "I know a filthy rich Godman by name Sasha in Bangalore who would buy our Opal."

They took a cab to Sasha's ashram. After reaching there, they were amazed to see his palace like luxurious ashram spread on hundreds of acres of land. They got into the ashram as his devotees. By seeing Ekong, one of the followers of Sasha allowed them to stay in a room in the ashram.

After settling down in the ashram, Alamayu asked Ekong, "Man, how do you know the Godman, Sasha."

He said, "I used to supply cocaine and other drugs to his ashram."

Alamayu wondered, "Why? The police don't take any action against him?"

Ekong said, "He has many policemen on his payroll. Even the city commissioner is his devotee. He also enjoyed political patronage as political parties depended on his innumerable followers' votes to win the election. No one can touch him. He owned hospitals, medical and engineering colleges. He also runs a drug and prostitution racket in his ashram. His hospitals are responsible for illegal organ trafficking. Sasha is worshiped as a demigod. His cult following is in millions extending even overseas. Sasha also claims to have supernatural powers.

Alamayu became curious, "He performs miracles?"

Ekong replied, "Yes, he could produce sacred ash (vibhuti) from air. At times, he performed levitation, made rocks explode by sprinkling holy water, he created fire by pouring ghee on wood. He used to carry flame on his palm in the form of burning camphor. On certain occasions, he walked on burning charcoal."

Alamayu asked Ekong, "If this man already possessed supernatural powers, why does he need our Ethiopian

Opal?"

Ekong smiled and said, "What Sasha performed where mere tricks and he doesn't have any supernatural powers."

Alamayu was surprised, "Tricks!"

Ekong explained, "Yes, the levitation trick is done by lying on the floor covered by a blanket and he slowly raises himself using two hockey sticks. He also levitated holding a stick and appeared floating above a mat supported only by bamboo stick held in his hand. The hollow bamboo stick and his robes contained a bracket which supported his weight and a rod runs through the bamboo which anchored hidden under the mat."

Alamayu asked, "How could Sasha walk on burning charcoal?"

Ekong said, "It is a simple trick. You just have to sprinkle salt on the coal which draws moisture or just wet your feet forming a layer of dirt on them. Then you just have to walk quickly to not get burned."

"Rest of the tricks were also easy like the rocks exploded on sprinkling holy water on them as the rocks contained sodium crystal in them which on reacting with ordinary water expands." Ekong said.

Alamayu asked, "What about burning camphor?"

Ekong said, "Burning camphor can be held in hand safely for a few seconds with some practice."

Mangestu asked, "What about his creating of fire by pouring ghee on wood?"

Ekong answered, "The wood contained potassium permanganate which reacts with glycerin like ghee and catches fire."

Alamayu asked, "Were you his assistant to have learnt all his tricks?"

Ekong smiled and said, "I was a street magician back in Nigeria before I turned into a drug peddler for the mafia. So, I am familiar with the tricks used by fake Godmen to fool the innocent people into believing that he had paranormal powers."

Godman Sasha called them to his chamber.

He said, "I would give you two million U.S. dollars for the Ethiopian Opal provided it has healing properties."

Alamayu said, "I will give you the Ethiopian Opal. You can test it on those who come for healing in the ashram. When you are sure of the Opal's healing properties, you hand over the money to us."

Sasha said, "Fine! Get me the opal and you can stay in the ashram cottage till I test the Opal's healing properties."

Alamayu handed over the Opal to Sasha. Godman Sasha tested its healing properties on sick people in the ashram. To his surprise, the Ethiopian fire Opal cured everybody of their diseases with its healing power including parkinsonism, blood disorders, eye problems, infection, fever, muscle disorders, spinal disorders etc. Impressed by its power, Godman Sasha gave them two million dollars, as promised.

Alamayu and Mangestu were happy that they finally got a deal for their Ethiopian Opal. They gave fifty percent of the share money to Ekong, as promised. Mangestu married Donna at the nearby church in Bangalore. Alamayu called his girlfriend Mahlet in Canada. She arranged for their airline tickets to Canada. Alamayu, Mangestu and Donna got on Jet airways to Delhi. From Delhi, they got on Air Canada and reached Vancouver in Canada in about eighteen hours' time span.

After reaching Canada, Alamayu sent plane tickets for his parents in Ethiopia to come to Canada. After his parents reached Canada, Alamayu took his father to Princess Margaret Cancer Center at Toronto for cancer treatment. In due course of time, Alamayu's father was fully cured of his lung cancer. Alamayu took his parents' and Mahlet's parents' permission and married Mahlet in their presence at Ethiopian Orthodox Tewahedo Church in Canada.

Alamayu and Mangestu started an Ethiopian restaurant in Toronto with the money they got by selling the Ethiopian opal. They got settled in Canada and led a happy life ever after.

*****